The Familiar

*A Classic Supernatural Tale of Dread
and Haunting Presence*

A Modern Translation

Adapted for the Contemporary Reader

J. Sheridan Le Fanu

Translated by Tim Zengerink

Table of Contents

Preface - Message to the Reader

What If You Could Help Rebuild the Greatest Library in Human History?

Thousands of years ago, the Library of Alexandria stood as the crown jewel of human achievement — a sanctuary where the collected wisdom of every known civilization was gathered, preserved, and shared freely.

And then, it was lost.

Through fire, conquest, and the slow erosion of time, humanity lost not just books — but ideas, dreams, discoveries, and stories that could have changed the world forever.

Today, the Library of Alexandria lives again — and you are invited to be a part of its restoration.

Our mission is simple yet profound:

To rebuild the greatest library the world has ever known, and to translate all timeless works into every language and dialect, so that no seeker of knowledge is ever left behind again.

By joining our movement to rebuild the modern Library of Alexandria, you become part of an unprecedented mission:

- **Unlimited Access to the Greatest Audiobooks & eBooks Ever Written:**

  Instantly explore thousands of legendary works— Plato, Shakespeare, Jane Austen, Leo Tolstoy, and countless more. All instantly available to read or listen, placing a complete literary universe at your fingertips.

- **Beautiful Paperback & Deluxe Editions at Printing Cost**

  Own any title as an elegant paperback, deluxe hardcover, or stunning collectible boxset—offered to you at true printing cost, delivered straight to your door. Build your personal Library of Alexandria, crafted for beauty, built for durability, and worthy of proud display.

- **Fresh Translations for Modern Readers—in Every Language & Dialect**

  Enjoy timeless masterpieces reimagined in clear, contemporary language—no more outdated phrases or obscure references. Alongside the original versions, we're tirelessly translating these classics into every language and dialect imaginable, ensuring accessibility and understanding across cultures and generations.

- **Join a Global Renaissance of Literature & Knowledge**

  You directly support expanding our library, publishing deluxe editions at true cost, translating works into all global languages, and bringing humanity's greatest stories to people everywhere. By joining today, you're not just preserving a legacy of masterpieces; you set in motion a powerful wave of literary accessibility.

Become a Torchbearer of Knowledge.

Join us for free now at **LibraryofAlexandria.com**

Together, we will ensure that the light of human wisdom never fades again.

With gratitude and a shared love of knowledge,

The Modern Library of Alexandria Team

Visit:

www.libraryofalexandria.com

Or scan the code below:

Introduction

Haunting Without End:
Guilt, Retribution, and the Shape That Follows

J. Sheridan Le Fanu's The Familiar stands among his most psychologically rich and atmospherically relentless ghost stories, a tale in which terror is not confined to the night or to the haunted house, but becomes a constant companion—stalking, echoing, and invading every corner of the protagonist's life. First published in 1872 in In a Glass Darkly, this novella-length tale is an expanded version of an earlier story titled The Watcher, but it is in this mature form that Le Fanu's exploration of dread reaches full power.

Set primarily in the gloomy streets of Dublin, The Familiar centers on Captain Barton, a disciplined, highly respected naval officer whose life is gradually consumed by a mysterious figure that seems to follow him everywhere. This entity—dwarfish, cloaked, and silent—is not merely a figment of fear, but the embodiment of something deeper: a force of judgment that cannot be escaped. The story unfolds not through sudden shocks, but through creeping inevitability, building a claustrophobic sense of doom that mirrors Barton's own psychological collapse.

What makes The Familiar so enduring is Le Fanu's refusal to explain too much. The titular being is never clearly identified. Is it a ghost? A demonic avenger? A projection of Barton's own repressed guilt? The answer lies not in the revelation of facts, but in the slow layering of atmosphere, tension, and the inexorable presence of the unseen. The figure that stalks Barton becomes, in a sense, a moral force—not of divine intervention, but of cosmic inevitability. In Le Fanu's world, the past does not rest. Wrongs are never truly forgotten. And the shadows that follow us do not always come from behind.

This introduction will offer a comprehensive examination of The Familiar—its structure, themes, characters, and place within Le Fanu's larger body of work. We'll explore the literary techniques that make the story so effective, the psychological landscape of Captain Barton, and the Victorian moral framework in which Le Fanu embeds his spectral tale. We'll also consider how the story helped shape the modern genre of the slow-burn haunting, and how its influence can be traced in works that blend mental disturbance with supernatural horror. The Familiar is not a tale of fright—it is a tale of fate, and the way fear tightens its grip not with a scream, but with a whisper.

The Shape of Guilt:
Captain Barton and the Burden of the Unconfessed

Captain Barton is introduced as a model of social virtue: a respected figure in both naval and Dublin society, outwardly confident and unshakable. Yet the early signs of unease appear almost immediately. Barton is restless. He walks alone at night. He reacts with visible agitation to certain sounds and glimpses. And most notably, he begins to speak of being followed. At first, it's subtle— a sense of being watched, of hearing footsteps that match his own. But soon, the presence becomes undeniable. He sees a short, hooded figure keeping pace with him through the city. He finds it waiting outside his home, following him from room to room, even appearing in his dreams.

Barton's descent is slow and realistic. Le Fanu is not interested in quick descent into madness; instead, he crafts a steady erosion of certainty, sanity, and safety. Barton tries to dismiss the figure as a delusion. He seeks advice, first from medical professionals, then from clergy. But none of it helps. The figure is not scared away by faith or rationality. It does not respond to confrontation. It simply is—a presence that observes, waits, and reminds.

The exact nature of the haunting is never fully disclosed, but hints accumulate throughout the narrative. Barton is haunted not randomly, but specifically. His fear is personal. He refers vaguely to a past transgression—something that happened during his service, something that might have involved betrayal, cruelty, or even death. The presence that stalks him, then, is not an external ghost. It is the embodiment of conscience, manifesting as something both outside and inside of him.

This is a classic Le Fanu theme: the intersection of the supernatural and the psychological. In The Familiar, horror is not just a matter of specters—it is rooted in moral decay. Barton's failure is not that he is weak, but that he has hidden the truth. And the story's great terror lies not in the figure's appearance, but in what it represents. It is not a stranger. It is known. It is deserved.

This allows the story to serve not only as a ghost story but as a moral allegory. Le Fanu uses Barton's fear to ask a larger question: what happens to guilt that is never confronted? What becomes of sins buried under status and silence? In this tale, they do not fade—they grow legs, don a cloak, and follow.

The Mechanics of Dread:
Le Fanu's Narrative Precision

Stylistically, The Familiar is a masterclass in atmospheric control. Le Fanu structures the story as a case study, filtered through the frame of Dr. Hesselius—a recurring character in his fiction who functions as a kind of spiritual detective. This framing device allows the story to move between testimony, observation, and inference, giving the reader multiple layers of distance. Rather than drawing the reader into immediate horror, Le Fanu makes us an observer of Barton's decline, which only intensifies the dread. We know the outcome. What grips us is the process.

The descriptions of the haunting are also meticulously restrained. The cloaked figure is seen only at a distance, often half-hidden, rarely interacting with Barton directly. Its power lies in its constancy. It never leaves. It never speaks. It appears in mirrors, windows, alleys, pews. Barton's own home becomes a trap—his rooms grow smaller, his sleep more fragmented, his nerves more frayed. The presence does not destroy him. It wears him down.

And then there are the dreams. Le Fanu infuses the narrative with surreal moments—visions of suffocation, death, the looming figure watching as Barton sleeps. These moments blur the line between waking and dreaming, leaving both Barton and the reader unsure of what is real. The horror is not in whether the figure exists, but in the certainty that Barton believes it does— and that he may be right.

This use of uncertainty is critical. Unlike more sensationalist ghost stories, The Familiar leaves space for interpretation. Is the figure real? Is it a projection of madness? Or is it something in between—a psychological manifestation with real-world effects? The answer, Le Fanu suggests, is less important than the experience of dread itself. Whether ghost or guilt, the thing that follows Barton cannot be outrun.

In this, Le Fanu anticipated a whole genre of horror rooted in unreliable perception, ambiguous hauntings, and the slow disintegration of identity. Writers from Henry James to Shirley Jackson to Stephen King have echoed this structure, and the influence of The Familiar is felt wherever horror is used to explore psychological trauma.

The Legacy of the Unseen:
Fate, Retribution, and the Gothic Tradition

The Familiar does not end with exorcism or clarity. It ends, instead, with silence. Captain Barton eventually dies under circumstances that are neither violent nor peaceful—his death is sudden, unexplained, and eerily calm. The figure is never caught or destroyed. It simply ceases to appear. The haunting is finished—not because justice has been served in a human sense, but because the debt has been collected.

This conclusion reflects Le Fanu's gothic vision of the universe: one in which spiritual forces operate according to rules we cannot fully grasp. Justice is not delivered by courts or clergy. It comes in shadows, in echoes, in things glimpsed from the corner of the eye. In this vision, sin is not forgotten. It is followed.

Le Fanu's particular genius lies in how he never fully demystifies the horror. He leaves gaps for the imagination to fill. In The Familiar, he invites us not to fear monsters—but to fear our own pasts. The figure that follows Barton is frightening not because it is monstrous, but because it is inevitable. It does not chase—it waits. It does not kill—it observes. It does not accuse—it reminds.

This is what makes the story so timeless. In a world filled with secrets, silences, and buried pain, The Familiar speaks to a universal fear: that what we thought we left behind is still with us. That there are things we did, or failed to do, that wait for us in quiet corners. And that when they finally step forward, it will be not to scream—but simply to stand beside us.

With The Familiar, J. Sheridan Le Fanu gave us one of the most haunting meditations on guilt and pursuit in all of literature. It is not about what hides in the dark. It is about what follows us in the light. And when we finally stop running, we may find it has already arrived.

Prologue

Out of about two hundred and thirty cases like the one I called "Green Tea," I've decided to share this one, which I've named "The Familiar."

As usual, Doctor Hesselius included a few extra pages of handwritten notes along with the manuscript. His writing is small and neat, almost like printed text. In his notes, he says:

"When it comes to honesty and trustworthiness, you couldn't ask for a better source than the elderly Irish clergyman who gave me this account of Mr. Barton's case. Still, from a medical standpoint, the report is incomplete. What's missing is the perspective of a skilled doctor who followed the patient's condition from start to finish. With that, I could make a much clearer judgment. I would also need to know if Mr. Barton had any inherited conditions or early warning signs that pointed to this illness before it became obvious.

In general, I group cases like this into three main categories, based on whether the experience is happening inside the person's mind or actually caused by something outside them. Some people just imagine things because of problems with their brain or nerves. Others really are affected by what we call 'spiritual beings' that are outside of themselves. Then there's a third group, who experience a mix of both—something is wrong inside, but that problem also opens a door to outside forces. It's kind of like when someone loses a layer of skin that normally protects them. Without it, they're left vulnerable to things that shouldn't be able to get in. In the brain, this might show up as a recurring disturbance in how blood flows through it. I've written more about this in my manuscript Essay A.17. These disturbances are different from regular pressure or swelling in the brain (which I explain in Essay A.19). When they're strong enough, they always come with hallucinations.

If I had been able to examine Mr. Barton myself, I'm confident I could've figured out exactly what was going on. But since I wasn't, I can only make an educated guess."

That's what Dr. Hesselius wrote. The rest of his notes are mostly of interest to doctors.

What follows is the written account by Reverend Thomas Herbert, which contains everything known about this case.

Chapter I.
Footsteps

I was a young man when this strange story happened, and I knew some of the people involved. The events made a deep impression on me, and I've never forgotten them. I'll do my best to tell the story clearly, adding in details I later learned from other sources, even if they don't fully explain everything that happened.

Around 1794, the younger brother of a certain baronet—let's call him Sir James Barton—came back to Dublin. This man, Captain Barton, had served in the navy with some success, even commanding one of His Majesty's frigates during most of the American war. He was about 42 or 43 years old, smart, and could be a pleasant person when he wanted to be, although he was usually quiet and sometimes moody.

Still, in public he acted like a true gentleman. He didn't have the loud or rough manners some men pick up at sea. Instead, he was calm and polite. He was medium height and fairly strong. His face showed signs of deep thought, and he generally looked serious, even sad. But being from a good family and having money, he easily entered the best social circles in Dublin.

Captain Barton didn't live in a flashy way. He rented rooms in a popular part of the city, owned only one horse, and had just one servant. Though people said he didn't believe in religion, he lived a quiet, moral life. He didn't gamble or drink and mostly kept to himself. He joined parties and events more to distract himself than to enjoy them or connect with others. Because of this, people thought he was a thrifty, serious man who would stay single, live a long life, and leave his money to a hospital.

But they were wrong. A young lady, whom I'll call Miss Montague, had just entered high society with her aunt, the Dowager Lady L—. Miss Montague was pretty, talented, and cheerful. She quickly became very popular, but that didn't help her much. She had no money, which made her less appealing to men looking for a wife. So when Captain Barton was suddenly seen courting her, everyone was surprised.

His proposal moved quickly. Lady L— soon told everyone that Captain Barton had asked to marry her niece and that Miss Montague had agreed, as long as her father approved. Her father was on his way back from India and was expected home in a few weeks. No one thought he would say no, so the couple was considered officially engaged. Following old traditions, Lady L— then took her niece out of the social scene completely.

Captain Barton became a regular visitor at the house and was treated like a future husband. Everything seemed to be going well, until strange things started to happen.

Lady L— lived in a grand home on the north side of Dublin, while Captain Barton's lodgings were on the south side. He usually walked home alone at night after visiting them. His usual route went through a long stretch of road where buildings were still under construction—just walls and foundations, no homes yet.

One night, not long after he got engaged, he stayed especially late. The conversation that evening had taken a serious turn. They discussed religion, and Barton had shown his disbelief in it. Back then, many wealthy and politically liberal people held similar views, so neither Lady L— nor her niece saw this as a serious problem.

The topic then shifted to ghosts and supernatural things. Barton continued to speak with the same mocking tone. He truly didn't believe in any of it. That was part of what made what happened next so strange: the man who would soon face something terrifying didn't believe such things could exist.

It was well after midnight when Captain Barton finally left to walk home. The moon was out, but the light was weak. The half-built street he walked through looked even more empty and lonely in that dim glow. The only sound was his footsteps, which echoed louder than usual in the quiet night.

After walking for a while, he suddenly heard another set of footsteps behind him, matching his pace about twenty steps back. The idea of being followed, especially in such a deserted place, was unsettling. He quickly turned around, expecting to see someone. But the road behind him was completely empty.

He tried stamping his foot and walking back and forth, thinking it might have just been an echo. But no sound bounced back. Though he wasn't the type to believe in the supernatural, the moment felt eerie. Still, he convinced himself it was just his imagination and kept walking.

But then, the footsteps started again. This time, they didn't just match his pace—they changed speed. Sometimes they slowed down, then suddenly hurried up, as if someone was running to catch up. Again, Barton spun around. Again, no one was there.

He even walked back over the same path, determined to find whoever—or whatever—was making the sound. But nothing appeared. His uneasiness grew stronger. Though he had never been afraid like this before, he couldn't shake the nervous feeling creeping over him.

He kept walking, but the footsteps returned at the same spot where they had started before. They came with bursts of speed, as if someone invisible was rushing toward him. Barton stopped and shouted loudly, "Who's there?"

The silence that followed was worse than the sound. Shouting into the empty night and getting no response felt deeply disturbing. He began to feel the urge to run, but his pride kept him walking steadily.

The strange steps followed him all the way to his home, and only when he was safe inside by his fire did he start to calm down. As he sat there, he tried to make sense of what had just happened. It was such a small thing—just footsteps—but it had completely shaken him. So much for being a proud skeptic. Sometimes, it only takes one strange moment to make us question everything we believe.

Chapter II.
The Watcher

Mr. Barton was eating a late breakfast the next morning, thinking more with curiosity than fear about what had happened the night before. The bright daylight had already started to wash away the spooky feelings. Just then, the mail arrived, and a letter was placed in front of him on the table.

At first glance, the envelope didn't look unusual, except for the handwriting, which was narrow and slanted backward—a style he didn't recognize. Maybe it had been purposely changed. Like many people do, he stared at the address for a while before opening it. Once he did, he found this message inside, written in the same odd handwriting:

'Mr. Barton, former captain of the Dolphin, is in danger. He should stay away from [the street he walked on last night]. If he goes there again, something bad will happen. This is a serious warning. He has a real reason to be afraid of THE WATCHER.'

Captain Barton read the letter again and again, turning it in every direction. He checked the paper and studied the handwriting. The wax seal showed nothing but a thumbprint. There were no names, no clues—nothing to tell him who had written it. It seemed to be a warning from someone trying to help, yet the writer claimed Barton had reason to fear him. The letter was deeply unsettling and reminded him of the strange footsteps the night before.

Though the events bothered him, Captain Barton didn't tell anyone—not even his fiancée. He thought she might take it as a sign of weakness, and he didn't want to seem foolish. Maybe the letter was just a prank, and maybe the footsteps had been some trick or illusion. He pretended not to care, but the thought of it all kept bothering him, and for some time afterward, he avoided the street mentioned in the warning.

About a week later, the strange memories had begun to fade. One night, Barton walked Miss Montague and Lady L— to their carriage after a theater performance. He hung back for a bit to chat with some friends, but parted ways near the college and headed home alone. It was around one in the morning, and the streets were completely empty.

While walking with his friends, he'd thought he heard footsteps following them. A few times, he looked back, hoping to spot someone and explain the sounds—but the streets had been empty.

Now, walking alone, the feeling returned stronger. He clearly heard footsteps matching his own pace along the wall of the college park. Just like before, the steps changed speed—sometimes fast, sometimes slow—like someone sneaking or rushing behind him. He turned around again and again, but saw no one.

The invisible presence wore down his nerves. By the time he reached home, he was so shaken that he couldn't sleep and didn't even lie down until the sun was up.

When his servant brought him the morning mail, one letter stood out immediately. The handwriting matched the warning he'd received before. It read:'

'You might as well try to outrun your own shadow, Captain Barton, as try to get away from me. I'll show up whenever I want, and you'll see me too—I'm not hiding. But don't let it bother you—if you haven't done anything wrong, there's no reason to be afraid of THE WATCHER.'

Reading this strange message left Barton badly shaken. He became noticeably quiet and distracted for days, though no one around him knew the reason. Whatever he thought about the mysterious footsteps, the letters were very real—and arriving so soon after the strange encounters made them even more disturbing.

The whole situation brought back memories Barton wanted to forget—moments in his past that filled him with regret or shame. Fortunately, he had more than his upcoming wedding to focus on. He was also involved in sorting out a large legal claim involving property, which kept him busy and helped lift the cloud of fear that had been hanging over him.

Still, now and then, the strange footsteps returned. He sometimes heard them faintly in quiet places—even in daylight. But they were less intense, less clear, and often he couldn't tell if he was imagining them or not.

One evening, Barton was walking to the House of Commons with a friend—someone I also knew. I happened to be with them. As we walked, I noticed Barton became distant and quiet, clearly troubled by something. Later, I learned that during that entire walk, he had heard the same footsteps stalking him once more.

That, however, was the last time he experienced the footsteps. But something new and even stranger was about to begin.

Chapter III.
An Advertisement

The new set of strange events that would later change Captain Barton's life began that same evening, though I wouldn't have remembered it if it hadn't been part of a bigger story.

As we were walking through the passage from College Green, a short man—he looked like a foreigner and wore a furry travel cap—rushed toward us. He looked very upset and was talking to himself quickly and angrily. He headed straight for Barton, who was walking slightly ahead of us. The man stopped in front of him for a few seconds, glaring with a wild, furious look, then turned sharply and walked away just as fast, disappearing down a side passage.

I remember being disturbed by the man's face—it gave me a weird, strong feeling of danger that I've never forgotten. But even though I was uneasy, it didn't really scare me. I just thought he looked like someone who might be mad or sick in the head.

But Barton's reaction shocked me. I knew him to be a brave and calm man, not one to panic. But when the man approached, Barton stepped back, grabbed my arm tightly, and looked completely terrified. When the man left, Barton suddenly pushed past me and followed him a few steps, then stopped in confusion and sat down looking pale and shaken. I'd never seen someone look so frightened.

"What's the matter, Barton?" one of our friends asked, clearly worried. "Are you okay? Are you feeling sick?"

"What did he say?" Barton asked instead, not even responding to the question. "I didn't catch it—what exactly did he say?"

"That guy?" our friend said. "Who cares what he said? Barton, you don't look good. Let me get you a carriage."

"I'm not sick," Barton replied, clearly trying to get himself under control. "I'm just tired and a little stressed. That lawsuit I've been dealing with is almost over, and it's been tough. I haven't felt right all night, but I'm okay now. Let's keep going."

"No, seriously, Barton, you should go home and rest," his friend said firmly. "You really don't look well. Let me walk you back."

I agreed with his friend, and Barton didn't argue much. He left us, saying he didn't need company. I didn't know the other man well enough to discuss what had just happened, but I could tell he was just as suspicious as I was that Barton's excuse wasn't the whole truth.

The next day I stopped by Barton's place to check on him. His servant told me he hadn't left his room since the night before but wasn't seriously ill. That same evening, Barton asked a well-known doctor, Dr. R---, to visit him. The doctor later described the visit as odd.

Barton explained his symptoms in a distracted way, as if he didn't really care about being cured. It was obvious that something else was on his mind. He said he had headaches and a racing heartbeat. The doctor asked if he was under any stress or worry. Barton quickly and sharply said no.

The doctor decided it was just a mild stomach issue and gave him a prescription. But just as he was about to leave, Barton suddenly remembered something.

"Wait, Doctor," he said. "I forgot—can I ask you a few weird medical questions? I've got a bet riding on the answers. Hope you don't mind."

The doctor agreed.

Barton was quiet for a moment, then said, "You'll think these are silly, but here goes. First, let's say someone has lockjaw. A real doctor thinks the person is dead from it. Is it possible they could still be alive and recover?"

The doctor smiled and shook his head. "No one who's actually seen a dead body could make that mistake in a case of lockjaw."

Barton thought for a moment. "Okay, how about this: say someone not trained in medicine makes the mistake. Could they confuse a stage of the illness with death?"

"Still no," the doctor replied. "Not if they've ever seen real death."

Barton paused again. "Alright, another one. Are foreign hospitals—like one in Naples—known for making sloppy mistakes with their records? Could they mix up names or lose track of patients?"

The doctor said he didn't know enough about that to say.

"Last one," Barton said. "Is there any disease, even a rare one, that could make a man shrink—make him shorter and smaller all over—but still look exactly the same in every other way? Same face, voice, everything but his size?"

The doctor said definitely not.

Then Barton asked quickly, "If someone is afraid of being attacked by a lunatic, can they get a warrant to have them arrested?"

The doctor said that was more of a legal question, but yes, a magistrate could issue a warrant if needed.

The doctor then left, but remembered he'd forgotten his cane upstairs. When he came back in, he awkwardly caught Barton burning the prescription he had just written, while sitting nearby looking very gloomy and scared. The doctor pretended not to notice, but he now believed Barton's real issue wasn't physical—it was mental.

A few days later, a strange ad appeared in the Dublin newspapers:

"If Sylvester Yelland, who once worked on His Majesty's ship the 'Dolphin,' or his closest relative, contacts Mr. Hubert Smith, attorney, in Dame Street, they may hear something very much in their favor. Inquiries can be made any time up to midnight, for privacy. All communication will be kept confidential."

The "Dolphin" was the ship Barton had commanded, and the unusual ad—along with how hard someone was trying to spread it—made the doctor suspect that Barton was behind it, and that this Yelland person was connected to whatever was troubling him.

But this was only a guess. No one, including the lawyer who placed the ad, gave any information about what it was really about or who had requested it.

Chapter IV.
He Talks with A Clergyman

Mr. Barton had recently started to seem like someone overly worried about his health, but that wasn't really true. He wasn't a cheerful person, but he normally had a steady mood and didn't often get sad or anxious.

Soon, he began returning to his usual habits. One sign that he was feeling better was that he attended a fancy dinner held by the Freemasons, a group he belonged to. At first, Barton seemed quiet and distant, but he drank more wine than usual—maybe to ease his hidden worries—and the cheerful company helped him relax. Before long, he was talking and laughing more than he usually did.

Feeling upbeat, Barton decided to stop by Lady L's house and spend the rest of the evening with her and his fiancée. He arrived in good spirits and enjoyed his visit. He hadn't had too much to drink—just enough to lift his mood without making him act out of line.

With his mood so high, he forgot all about the fears and anxiety that had been troubling him for so long. But as the night went on and his excitement faded, those dark thoughts slowly returned, and he started to feel nervous and distracted again.

When he finally said goodbye and left, he had a strange sense that something bad was going to happen. He tried to ignore these fears, telling himself they were foolish, even though they weighed heavily on his mind.

It was this stubborn denial of fear that pushed him to make the decision that led to the next strange event. He could have easily called for a carriage, but he knew the only reason he wanted one was because of his nervousness. He could've also taken a different path home, instead of the one he had been warned about. But again, he refused. Determined to face whatever was coming—if anything at all—he chose to walk the exact same route he had taken on the night when all these strange events had first begun.

Still, walking that dark path took every bit of courage he had. Barton moved quickly, barely breathing from the tension, but for a while, everything stayed quiet. The creepy footsteps he had feared never came, and as he neared the edge of the deserted area—where the city lights began—he started to feel relieved.

That relief didn't last long.

Suddenly, a gunshot rang out behind him, and a bullet flew just past his head. Barton froze in shock. His first instinct was to turn back and find the shooter, but he quickly realized that it was hopeless. The area was surrounded by empty lots and half-built buildings, with piles of rubble and old brick kilns. Everything was still and silent. There was no one around and no sound of footsteps or movement.

Realizing he was alone and that searching would do no good, Barton turned again and hurried toward home. He didn't run, but his steps were fast and tense. His heart pounded with the shock of barely escaping death.

As Captain Barton turned to walk away, just moments after the gunshot, he suddenly came face-to-face with the small man in the fur cap—the same one he had seen before. The encounter lasted only a few seconds. The man was moving quickly and had the same strange, threatening energy as last time. As he passed Barton, he thought he heard him whisper angrily, "Still alive, still alive!"

Barton's state of mind had started to affect his health and appearance. The change was so obvious that everyone around him noticed. But for reasons only he knew, Barton told no one about the attempt on his life. He didn't report it to the authorities, and he didn't speak of it at all until several weeks later, when he confided in a single trusted person.

Despite his troubled thoughts, Barton still had to show the world a cheerful and confident face—especially since he was engaged to Miss Montague. He had no good excuse for pulling away from her or from his social obligations, so he forced himself to keep up appearances. But the truth behind his suffering remained tightly guarded, and it seemed as though he knew more than he let on—like he understood what was happening but couldn't or wouldn't reveal it.

This constant fear, locked inside and left unspoken, began to consume him. It made his nerves more sensitive and his imagination more vulnerable. Because of this, he started to experience more frequent and terrifying visits from the strange figure that had haunted him since the beginning.

Around this time, Barton went to visit a well-known preacher he barely knew. The preacher was deep in study when Barton arrived. The moment Barton entered the room, his pale face and anxious look made it clear that something had deeply disturbed him.

After the usual polite greetings and small talk, Barton saw that the preacher was surprised by his visit. Barton broke the silence by saying, "I know this is an unusual visit, especially since we barely know each other.

Normally, I wouldn't disturb you—but I'm in serious trouble. I need help."

The preacher responded kindly, encouraging him to speak freely. Barton continued, "I'm here to ask for your advice—and your compassion—because I've been going through something terrible."

"My dear sir," said the preacher, "I'll gladly help however I can, especially if it brings you peace of mind."

"I know what you're thinking," Barton said quickly. "You think I'm an unbeliever, and that religion won't help me. But don't assume that. My beliefs may be shaky, but recent events have forced me to think about faith more seriously than I ever have before."

The preacher suggested, "So, your questions are about whether religious teachings are true?"

"Not exactly," Barton replied. "I haven't even sorted out my own objections yet. But there's one topic that really matters to me."

He paused, and the preacher encouraged him to go on.

"The truth is," Barton said, "whether or not the Bible is real, I'm convinced of one thing—there is a spiritual world. Usually, we're protected from seeing it. But sometimes, it reveals itself—and it's terrifying. I know there's a God—a powerful, fearsome God—and I believe punishment comes to the guilty in ways we can't understand, through forces that are terrifying and beyond explanation. I'm sure of it—absolutely sure. I've felt it myself. There's something evil, unstoppable, and full of hate that has targeted me. I'm suffering like someone already in hell. The pain, the fear—it's unbearable."

As Barton spoke, his fear became overwhelming. His voice sped up, his face twisted with terror, and the preacher could see how deeply this man—usually calm and composed—was now falling apart.

Chapter V.
Mr. Barton States His Case

"My dear friend," said the doctor after a short pause, "it's clear you've been deeply upset. But I really think your sadness is caused by something physical. With some fresh air, healthy food, and a few simple treatments, your mood will improve, and your mind will feel steady again. People used to believe that our emotions were connected to how our bodies worked—and there's more truth to that than we like to admit. I truly believe you'll feel like yourself again with a little care."

Captain Barton shivered a little. "Doctor," he said, "I can't lie to myself like that. I only have one hope left—some greater power, something stronger than whatever's haunting me, might be able to fight it off. If not, then I'm completely lost—forever."

"But others have been through terrible things too," the doctor said gently, "and—"

"No, no, no," Barton interrupted, growing more upset. "I'm not easily fooled. I'm not the kind of person who believes in ghosts or magic. If anything, I've always been too doubtful. But now, unless I want to ignore everything I've seen and heard—even with my own eyes and ears—I have to admit the truth. I'm being followed. Haunted. No matter where I go, something evil is after me."

The fear on Barton's face was enough to make anyone uneasy—his skin pale, his eyes wide with dread.

"God help you," the doctor said, truly shaken. "Whatever the cause, you're clearly suffering."

"Yes, yes—God help me," Barton said again, but without hope. "But will He? That's what I need to know."

"You must pray to Him," the doctor replied. "Pray with trust in your heart."

"Pray?" Barton repeated, sounding hollow. "I can't. Asking me to pray is like asking me to move a mountain. I don't have enough faith. Something inside me won't let me. You're asking me to do the impossible."

"You might not find it so hard if you just try," the doctor encouraged him.

"I have tried!" Barton shouted. "But every time, it just makes me feel lost—or terrified. I've failed. Just thinking about God—about forever and never-ending time—makes my head spin. I can't handle it. I panic. If

I'm going to be saved, it won't be through prayer. The very thought of an eternal Creator is too much for me."

"Then tell me how I can help," said the doctor softly. "Tell me what I can say or do to give you some peace."

"Listen to me first," Barton said, calming himself down. "Let me tell you what's been happening—what's made life feel like a nightmare. I'm terrified of dying and what might come next, but I hate being alive just as much."

He began to tell the doctor everything—every detail of the haunting. Then he added:

"This happens all the time now. It's part of my life. I don't see him every day, thank God. At least I've been given a little peace there. But I can always feel him close by, always watching. I hear his voice, filled with rage, yelling at me. On the street, in my room at night—he's always there. He screams that I've committed horrible sins. He says I'll be punished, that I'm going to hell. Wait! Do you hear that?" Barton suddenly cried, a twisted smile on his face. "There—right there! Do you believe me now?"

The clergyman felt a cold chill run through him. As a strong gust of wind rushed by, he thought he heard angry, mocking whispers mixed into the sound—or maybe it was just his imagination.

"Well, what do you make of that?" Barton finally asked, breathing sharply through his teeth.

"I heard the wind," said the doctor. "What's so strange about it?"

"The prince of the powers of the air," Barton muttered with a shiver.

"Nonsense, my dear sir," the doctor replied, trying to shake off his own uneasiness. It was still daylight, but Barton's nervous energy was starting to affect him, too. "You can't give in to these wild thoughts. You have to fight back against these tricks of the mind."

"Yes, yes—'resist the devil, and he will flee from you,'" Barton said in the same trembling voice. "But how do I resist him? That's the problem—what am I supposed to do? What can I do?"

"This is just your imagination," said the doctor, trying to sound firm. "You're tormenting yourself."

"No, sir. This isn't imagination," Barton replied, more firmly now. "Was it imagination that made both of us hear that voice just now? No. That was real. That was something from hell."

"But if you've seen this person so often," the clergyman asked, "why haven't you tried speaking to him—or at least catching him? Isn't it a bit extreme to say this is something supernatural? Maybe there's a normal explanation if we just investigate properly."

"There are things about this… thing… that I can't explain, but that prove to me it's not human," Barton said. "I know it's something evil. I could make you believe it, too, if you saw what I've seen."

He paused for a moment, then added, "And as for talking to it—I can't. I freeze up. When I see it, I feel like I'm staring straight at death. I feel trapped, like I'm facing pure evil. My strength, my thoughts—everything leaves me. You don't know what you're talking about. Please… have mercy. May heaven have mercy on me!"

He leaned his elbow on the table and covered his eyes with his hand, as if trying to block out something terrifying. He whispered the last words again and again like a prayer.

"Doctor," he suddenly said, sitting upright and staring at the clergyman with pleading eyes, "I know you'll help me, if there's anything that can be done. Now that you understand everything—now that you see what I'm going through—I beg you: if there's anything, anything at all, that can be done to help me— through prayer, through the intercession of good people, through some kind of holy help—I'm asking you, in the name of God, please use that power. Save me from this horror. Fight for me. Have pity. That's why I came to you. Just give me some hope, even a tiny bit—just something to hold on to. If you can do that, I'll try to bear this nightmare my life has become."

The doctor promised he would pray for Barton with all his heart, and said that was the most he could do.

They said goodbye quickly and sadly. Barton hurried out to the carriage waiting for him, pulled down the blinds, and rode away. The doctor went back to his study, left alone to think over the strange and disturbing visit.

Chapter VI.
Seen Again

People quickly noticed the strange changes in Captain Barton's behavior, and many began to talk about it. Some thought he was secretly having money problems. Others believed he was trying to get out of an engagement he regretted. But the most common explanation was that he was starting to lose his mind.

Miss Montague, who was engaged to Barton, noticed the change early on. Because they were close, and because she cared deeply, she paid close attention to his behavior. Over time, his visits became rare and when he did show up, he seemed distracted, tense, and nervous. Lady L——, her aunt, finally spoke up. After dropping hints for a while, she directly asked Barton what was wrong.

He told them the truth. At first, his explanation made them feel better—it didn't sound like anything too terrible. But the more they thought about it, the more disturbed they became. His words hinted at something deeply troubling and possibly dangerous to both his mental health and his spirit.

Soon after, Miss Montague's father, General Montague, returned from abroad. He had known Barton a little years ago and thought he would be a perfect match for his daughter. He didn't take Barton's story seriously and went to visit him right away.

"My dear Barton," the General said jokingly, "I hear you've gotten scared of ghosts in a brand new way."

Barton sighed heavily, clearly upset.

"Come now," the General continued, "you look more like a man heading to his execution than to a wedding. These devils of yours have made a saint out of you."

Barton tried to change the subject.

"No, no, I must say what I came to say," the General insisted with a smile. "You can't be serious. A full-grown man scared by some spooky little figure in a red vest and a bad face? It's ridiculous. I'm sure we can figure out who this is in no time."

"You don't know the full story," Barton said quietly.

"Oh, but I know enough," the General replied. "You keep seeing this small man who appears out of nowhere, and it rattles you. I'll find him, beat him senseless myself, or have him dragged through town for being such a pest."

"If you knew what I know," Barton said, visibly shaken, "you wouldn't speak so lightly. I have reasons—serious ones—for believing what I do. The proof is right here." He tapped his chest and sighed, pacing nervously.

"Well," said the General, "I still bet I'll catch your ghost and prove it's just a regular man."

He was about to continue when Barton suddenly stepped back from the window in shock. His face turned white as snow. He pointed outside and muttered, "There—by heaven—there he is!"

The General jumped up and looked out. He saw someone that matched the description—leaning by the rail, just starting to turn away. Without hesitation, the General grabbed his cane and hat and rushed out the door.

He searched the area quickly but couldn't find the man. He ran to the street corner and scanned every direction. No figure, no movement—nothing. Strangers passing by began to stare and laugh at the sight of the frantic older man waving his cane, which made him realize how ridiculous he must have looked. Embarrassed, he straightened his hat, lowered his cane, and walked back to Barton's house.

Barton was still inside, shaking and pale. The two men sat quietly for a while—Barton from fear, the General from frustration.

"You saw him?" Barton finally whispered.

"Yes—I saw someone," said the General, annoyed. "But what good is that? He vanished like smoke. Next time, though, if I get near him, I'll give him something to remember."

Despite the General's confidence, nothing changed. Barton still saw the mysterious figure everywhere he went. It followed him constantly, appearing in streets, around corners—anywhere, at any time. The stress wore him down. His health started to suffer, and his mind seemed on edge.

Lady L— and the General finally convinced Barton to take a short trip through Europe, hoping that new surroundings might break the mental pattern causing all this. His friends who didn't believe in ghosts thought the change in scenery might distract him from his fears, which they believed were just the result of stress and imagination.

But the General himself believed the figure was real—a flesh-and-blood man with a personal grudge against Barton, possibly even planning to hurt him. This idea wasn't much more comforting, but the General thought that if Barton could just realize that the figure wasn't supernatural, he might stop being so afraid, and start feeling like himself again.

If Barton could get far enough away and the sightings stopped, it would prove that this haunting wasn't anything beyond the natural world.

Chapter VII.
Flight

Barton finally gave in to the urging of his friends and left Dublin for England, accompanied by General Montague. They traveled quickly to London, then to Dover, and finally took a ship to Calais with a smooth wind at their back. Since leaving Ireland, Barton hadn't had a single episode—no sign, real or imagined, of the terrifying figure that had haunted him for so long. This brought him an enormous sense of relief. He began to feel hope again and even dreamed of a future that, just a short while ago, he had been too afraid to imagine.

He and Montague both quietly believed the nightmare was over. They were sure the change of scenery had broken whatever terrible spell had hung over Barton.

It was a lovely day when they arrived, and a crowd had gathered on the pier to watch the ship come in. Montague was walking ahead through the crowd when a short man with a thick accent tapped his arm and said, "Sir, you're walking too fast. You'll lose your sick friend—he looks like he's going to faint."

Montague spun around and saw that Barton did, in fact, look ghostly pale. He rushed back to him. "Are you feeling alright?"

It took Barton a moment to respond. Then, barely able to speak, he muttered, "I saw him. I swear I saw him!"

"Saw who? That man? Where is he now?" Montague asked, scanning the crowd.

"He's gone," Barton said faintly.

"Gone? But where? What did he look like? What was he wearing?" Montague asked in a rush, ready to chase after the figure.

"He touched your arm. He pointed to me. God help me—there's no escape," Barton whispered, looking completely broken.

Montague pushed through the crowd, furious and determined to catch the man. He clearly remembered what he looked like—but he couldn't find anyone that even came close. He even got help from people nearby, who thought he had been robbed, but the man had vanished.

Montague finally gave up, breathing heavily. "My friend," Barton said quietly, pale and dazed, "it's no use.

I can't fight this. Whatever it is, it's part of me now. I'll never be free."

"Don't say that," Montague replied, both worried and annoyed. "We'll deal with this. Don't give up."

But from that moment on, Barton lost all hope. It didn't matter what anyone said—he had given up. His mind, body, and spirit were all crumbling under the stress. He no longer had any will to make decisions, so he simply did whatever his closest friends advised.

They decided to take him to Lady L—'s house near Clontarf. His doctor still believed it was all caused by a nervous condition. The plan was to keep him indoors, only using rooms that looked out on a private courtyard. The gates were locked to make sure he wouldn't accidentally see someone who might remind him of the figure he feared so much.

His doctors hoped that by avoiding all possible triggers for a while—about a month or so—Barton's nerves might calm down. Friends and family would visit often, and everyone hoped that this break from the haunting routine might help him heal.

So Barton moved into the house, joined by Lady L—, General Montague, and Miss Montague, his fiancée. Barton himself had no hope left, but he went along with the plan without argument.

At first, it seemed like the plan was working. His health and spirits slowly began to improve, though he still looked like a shadow of the man he once was. His recovery was far from complete, but his small signs of progress brought happiness to those around him— especially to Miss Montague, who still deeply cared for him and was caught in a painful, uncertain position.

Weeks passed. Then a full month. Still, there was no sign of the mysterious figure. The plan seemed to be working. The mental chain had been broken. Barton began to reconnect with the world. He wasn't joyful, but he seemed less lost.

It was around this time that something strange happened. Lady L—, who prided herself on her knowledge of old remedies, sent her maid to the garden to gather herbs for a homemade medicine. But the maid came back early, clearly shaken. Her explanation for why she had returned so suddenly was strange—and it deeply disturbed the old lady.

Chapter VIII.
Softened

She had gone to the kitchen garden like her mistress told her to and started picking out the herbs she was supposed to gather. The plants were overgrown and messy, but she didn't seem to mind. As she worked, she casually sang part of an old song, just to keep herself company. But her singing was suddenly cut off by a mean, mocking laugh. When she looked up, she saw a strange, unpleasant-looking little man standing just outside the garden, staring at her through the thorny hedge. His face looked angry and threatening.

She said she couldn't move or speak, frozen in fear, while the man gave her a message to pass on to Captain Barton. He told her that Barton needed to start going outside again and being seen by his friends, or else he should get ready for a visit in his own room.

After delivering this chilling message, the man stepped into the ditch outside the fence and grabbed the thorny branches like he was about to climb through. It wouldn't have been hard for him to do it.

The girl didn't wait to see what would happen next. Dropping the herbs she had picked, she ran back to the house as fast as she could. Lady L ordered her not to speak a word about what happened, threatening to fire her if she did. She also sent her men to search the garden and the nearby fields, but, as usual, they found nothing. Still, Lady L felt deeply uneasy and decided to tell her brother about it. The story stayed between them for a long time, and they made sure Barton never heard about it. Meanwhile, he kept slowly getting better.

Eventually, Barton began walking around the courtyard, which was surrounded by high walls and didn't offer any view of the outside. Because of this, he felt safe there. A wooden gate led to the road, and outside of that was a locked iron gate. Barton had given clear instructions to always keep both gates locked. But one day, because a groom wasn't careful, something terrifying happened. As Barton reached the far end of the courtyard and turned around, he noticed the small wooden gate slightly open—and beyond the iron bars, the face of the same man who had haunted him before, staring straight at him. Barton froze in shock and fear, unable to move or breathe. Then he collapsed onto the ground, unconscious.

A few minutes later, someone found him and carried him back to his room. He would never leave that room again. From then on, something strange and hard to explain changed inside him. He wasn't frantic or desperate anymore. Instead, he became eerily calm, as if he already knew he was close to death.

"Montague, my friend, the end is near," he said quietly, with a serious and haunted look. "At last, I've been given some comfort from the spirit world—the place where this punishment came from. I now know that it won't be long."

Montague encouraged him to say more.

"Yes," Barton replied in a softer tone. "It's almost over. Maybe I'll never be free from sadness, even after death, but the pain is ending. I've been shown some peace, and I'm ready to face what's left with patience—even with hope."

"I'm glad to hear you speaking so calmly," Montague said. "Peace of mind is all you need to be yourself again."

"No," Barton said with quiet sorrow. "I'll never be that person again. I don't belong in the world of the living anymore. I'm going to die soon. I'm supposed to see him one last time—and then it'll all be over."

"He told you that?" Montague asked.

"Him? No—good news wouldn't come from him. What I heard came in a different way—gentle, full of love and sadness. I can't explain it all without bringing up old memories and people best left alone." As Barton said this, tears rolled down his cheeks.

"Come on," Montague said, misunderstanding his emotions. "You can't fall apart now. It's probably just dreams or some trick. Or maybe it's some sneaky guy who's mad at you and enjoys messing with your head— too much of a coward to do anything openly."

"Yes, he definitely holds a grudge against me," Barton said suddenly, shivering. "You're right to call it that. But it's more than that—it's terrifying. When Heaven allows evil to carry out revenge—when the task is given to someone who's already lost, someone ruined by sin, and that person was destroyed by the very man he's now told to haunt—that's when hell itself seems to come to Earth. But Heaven has shown me some mercy. I've found hope at last. If only I didn't have to see that horrible face again, I'd welcome death right now. I'm not afraid to die—but I'm terrified, truly terrified, of seeing him one last time. I know I will. And when I do, it'll be even worse than before."

As Barton spoke, he shook so hard that Montague became seriously worried and tried to change the subject, hoping to calm him down again.

"It wasn't a dream," Barton said after a pause. "I felt different, like I was in another world—but everything seemed just as real as what I see and hear now. It actually happened."

"What did you see and hear?" Montague asked gently.

"When I woke up after fainting at the sight of him," Barton said, ignoring the question directly, "it was very slow. I found myself lying beside a wide, calm lake, surrounded by foggy hills. A soft, sad, rosy light filled the air. It was lonely, but so beautiful—more beautiful than anything I've ever seen in this world. My head was resting on a girl's lap. She was singing a song that, somehow, told the whole story of my life—everything I've been through and everything that's still ahead. I don't know if it was the words or the music, but it all came rushing back to me—memories and emotions I thought were long gone. I started to cry—partly because of the song, and partly because her voice was so heartbreakingly sweet. And I knew that voice. I knew it well. But I couldn't turn to look at her. The moment was too powerful, too magical. I just listened and watched the quiet scene around me without moving, barely breathing. Then, slowly, the song and the view faded away, until everything was dark and silent again. When I came back to this world, I felt peace. I knew I had been forgiven for a lot."

Barton cried again, deeply and for a long time.

From that point on, his usual mood was one of quiet sadness. But even that calm was often broken. He believed with all his heart that one last, final visit was still waiting for him—something even more terrifying than anything he had gone through before. The fear of this unknown moment sometimes hit him so hard, he would fall into fits of panic and terror that scared everyone in the house. Even the people who claimed not to believe in ghosts or evil forces started to feel uneasy, especially late at night, though they never admitted it. No one tried to talk Barton out of staying in his room all the time. He completely shut himself in.

The blinds in his room were always closed, and his personal servant was never far from him, day or night. The servant even slept in the same room.

This man was loyal and trustworthy. Besides his usual work, he had to make sure Barton's simple safety steps were followed—small things, like making sure no windows or doors were open where "the Watcher" might appear. More than anything, Barton could not be left alone. Even one minute by himself was unbearable to him now. The idea of being alone scared him just as much as going outside in public. It was as if he could sense that something awful was about to happen.

Chapter IX.
Requiescat

Of course, given everything that had happened, there was no chance that Barton would go through with the engagement he had agreed to. The age difference and the difference in lifestyle between him and the young woman had always made it unlikely that she felt any deep or romantic love for him. Though she was sad and worried, she was far from heartbroken.

Miss Montague, however, spent much of her time trying to comfort Barton, even though her efforts made little difference. She read to him and tried to talk with him, but it was clear that nothing could distract him from the fear that haunted him constantly.

Like many young women, Miss Montague loved animals, and one of her pets was an old owl. A gardener had caught it sleeping in the ivy-covered ruins of an old stable and gave it to her as a gift. For some reason, she became very fond of this serious-looking and rather odd bird. It might seem like a silly detail, but this strange attachment to the owl plays a part in how the story ends.

Barton, on the other hand, absolutely hated the bird. From the moment he first saw it, he had a strong and strange fear of it. He couldn't even stand being near it. His fear was so intense and unreasonable that others almost laughed, not understanding how real it felt to him.

Now that this background is clear, here's what happened during the final, most disturbing event of all.

It was nearly two o'clock on a cold winter night. Barton was in bed, as usual, with his servant sleeping in a smaller bed nearby. A candle was lit in the room. Suddenly, Barton woke his servant and said, "I can't shake the feeling that the cursed bird got into the room somehow. I dreamed about it. Please get up and look around. The dreams were awful."

The servant got up and began checking the room. As he searched, he heard a strange, breathy sound— more like a deep sigh than a hiss—coming from the hallway outside the bedroom. This eerie noise, typical of owls, made him think the bird might actually be out there. So, he opened the door and stepped into the hallway to chase it away.

But just as he moved forward, the door behind him quietly swung shut. It seemed like it was just a breeze, and since there was a small window above the door letting out the candlelight, he could still see into the room.

As he walked down the hallway, he heard Barton calling his name from the bed, asking him to place the candle on the bedside table. Apparently, Barton didn't realize the servant had already left the room. Wanting to keep quiet so he wouldn't wake anyone else, the servant turned back, walking quickly and silently.

Then something shocking happened.

He heard someone inside the room answer Barton's request in a calm voice. Looking through the small window above the door, he saw the candlelight moving—as if someone was carrying it across the room. Frozen in fear but curious, the servant stood outside the door, too scared to go back in.

Then he heard the soft rustle of curtains and the gentle murmur of someone whispering, like a person trying to soothe a child to sleep. Through that sound, he heard Barton whisper in a horrified voice, "Oh God—oh, my God," over and over again.

Everything went quiet for a moment.

Then the quiet whispering returned, but it was followed by a loud, terrible scream—full of pain and terror. It was so horrifying that the servant, overcome with panic, threw himself at the door, trying with all his strength to break it open. Whether he had forgotten to turn the handle properly or if the door was locked from the inside, he couldn't get in. As he struggled, the awful screams kept coming, louder and more desperate, while that soft whispering sound continued behind them.

Shaking with fear and unsure of what to do, the servant finally gave up and ran down the hallway, wringing his hands in terror. At the top of the stairs, he ran into General Montague, who looked frightened and rushed. Just as they met, the screams inside the room suddenly stopped.

"What happened? Where's your master?" Montague asked, his voice shaking with fear. "Is something wrong? Please, tell me!"

"God help us, it's over," the servant said, staring in shock toward the bedroom. "He's dead, sir. I know he is."

Montague didn't wait for more explanation. With the servant right behind him, he rushed to the bedroom door, turned the handle, and pushed it open. As the door swung in, the owl—the one they had been looking for—suddenly flew out from behind the bed. It let out its eerie cry as it soared over their heads, blew out Montague's candle as it passed, then crashed through the skylight above the hallway and disappeared into the dark night.

"There it goes. God bless us," the servant whispered after a moment of silence.

"Curse that bird," muttered the General, clearly shaken by what had just happened.

"The candle was moved," the servant said after a pause, pointing at the one still burning inside the room. "Someone put it by the bed."

"Pull the curtains back," Montague whispered sharply. "Don't just stand there staring."

The man hesitated.

"Here, take this," Montague said, handing him the candlestick and stepping forward himself. He pulled the curtains open.

The candlelight revealed Barton's body, hunched over and half-sitting at the top of the bed. It looked like he had backed into the headboard as far as possible. His hands were still tightly gripping the blankets.

"Barton! Barton!" Montague cried out, filled with a mix of fear and desperation. He took the candle and held it so the light fell directly on Barton's face. His expression was frozen—stern, pale, and lifeless. His jaw hung slack, and his eyes, wide open, stared blankly toward the end of the bed.

"My God… he's dead," Montague whispered.

They both stared in silence for a long moment.

"He's cold, too," Montague said quietly, pulling his hand away from the dead man.

"Look, sir—look there!" the servant said, shivering. "Something else was on the bed with him. Look at that dent!"

He pointed to a deep indentation near the foot of the bed, as if something heavy had been sitting there.

Montague didn't respond.

"Let's go, sir. Please," the servant whispered, clinging to him and looking around nervously. "There's nothing more we can do. Please, let's get out of here."

At that moment, they heard footsteps approaching. Montague told the servant to stop them from coming in. Then he gently tried to loosen Barton's stiff grip on the blankets and lay him back on the bed. Once the body was resting more naturally, he drew the curtains shut again and left the room to meet the others.

What happened after that isn't important to this story. All that matters is that no explanation for the strange events was ever found. Years have passed since that terrible night, and still, no answers have come to light. Whatever secrets were behind it all remain hidden, and may never be known—at least not until all secrets of the world are finally revealed.

There was only one moment from Captain Barton's past that anyone ever mentioned as possibly connected to his terrible end. And even that story didn't come out until several years after his death. What was revealed was deeply upsetting to his family and damaging to his reputation.

It turned out that about six years before he returned to Dublin for the last time, Barton had a secret and shameful relationship with a young woman in Plymouth. She was the daughter of one of his crew members. Her father treated her cruelly when he found out, and some said she died of a broken heart.

Because Barton was involved, the father openly insulted him. Barton, furious at both the man's behavior and the way he had treated the girl, used his authority to punish him harshly. He used every cruel measure allowed by navy rules. Eventually, while the ship was docked in Naples, the man escaped. He later died in a hospital there from wounds he got during one of Barton's brutal punishments.

Whether these events had anything to do with what happened to Barton later, no one can say for sure. But it's very likely that Barton himself believed they were connected. Whatever the truth is, the things that haunted and destroyed Barton will probably remain a mystery forever.

The End

Thank You for Reading

Dear Reader,

We hope this timeless classic has sparked your imagination and enriched your literary journey. Now that you've turned the final page, we want to share a vision for the future of reading—one where every classic you've ever wanted to explore is at your fingertips, in a format that best suits your life.

We'd like to invite you to gain immediate, unlimited digital & audiobook access to hundreds of the most treasured literary classics ever written—along with the option to secure deluxe paperback, hardcover & box set editions at printing cost. Together, we can spark a new global literary renaissance alongside our small, independent publishing house called "The Library of Alexandria."

Thousands of years ago, the Library of Alexandria stood as a beacon of knowledge—until it was lost to history. We aim to reignite that spirit of preservation and discovery right now, in the modern age—only this time, it's accessible to all, in every language and every format.

Picture a world where every timeless classic, novel, poem, or philosophical treatise is not only available to read but also updated for today's readers—modernized, translated into any language or dialect, and ready to enjoy in any format you choose, whether that is in an eBook, audiobook, paperback, or deluxe hardcover & box set version a printing cost.

By joining our movement to rebuild the modern Library of Alexandria, you become part of an unprecedented mission to offer:

- **Unlimited Audiobook & eBook Access to the Greatest Classics of All Time**

  Instantly explore thousands of legendary works, from Plato and Shakespeare to Jane Austen and Leo Tolstoy. All are instantly ready to read or listen to, giving you a complete literary universe at your fingertips.

- **Paperback & Deluxe Editions at Printing Costs:**

  Purchase any title in a paperback, deluxe hardbound, or deluxe boxset edition at printing costs, shipped right to your doorstep. Curate your personal library of Alexandria with editions worthy of display— crafted to last, designed to captivate, and delivered straight to your door.

- **Modern translations for Contemporary Readers in all languages and dialects**

  Discover a vast selection of classics reimagined in clear, current language—no more struggling with outdated phrases or obscure references. Next to the original versions, we aim to offer translations in as many languages and dialects as possible.

  As we continue our translation efforts and add new languages, readers everywhere can connect with these works as if they were written today. By bridging linguistic divides, you're contributing to ensuring that these timeless stories become more meaningful, accessible, and inspiring for people across the globe.

- **Your Personal Library of Alexandria:**

  Over the months and years, you'll curate a unique physical archive of classics—each volume a testament to your taste, curiosity, and love of knowledge. It's not just about owning books—it's about curating a cultural legacy you'll cherish and pass down for generations to come.

- **Join a Global Literary Renaissance:**

  Your support fuels an ongoing mission: allowing us to reinvest in offering deluxe print editions (including special boxsets) at their true cost, broaden the range of available formats and translations, and extend the reach of these works to new audiences worldwide. By joining today, you're not just preserving a legacy of masterpieces; you set in motion a powerful wave of literary accessibility.

We are more than a publisher—we're a movement, and we can't do it alone. Your support lets us scale our mission, preserving and reimagining history's greatest works for tomorrow's readers.

Become a Torchbearer of knowledge.

Thank you for picking up this book and allowing us into your literary journey. As you turn the pages, know that you're part of something larger: a global effort to keep these stories alive, share their wisdom across borders and generations, and spark a true cultural revival for the modern era.

If this resonates with you—please consider taking the next step by visiting:

www.libraryofalexandria.com

With gratitude and a shared love of knowledge,

The Modern Library of Alexandria Team

Visit:

www.libraryofalexandria.com

Or scan the code below:

www.ingramcontent.com/pod-product-compliance
Lightning Source LLC
Chambersburg PA
CBHW011453260626
47154CB00018B/2973